Grandmother's Bell
And The Wagon Train
1849

For Johnny and Crystal

Grandmother's Bell
And The Wagon Train
1849

By Joan Barton Barsotti

Illustrated by Carol Mathis

Barsotti Publishing Co.
Camino, California

Grandfather stood beside the wagon, looking at the mountains. They were huge! Grandfather and his family were going to California and they had to go across those mountains to get there. It would not be easy.

Grandfather sighed. "The wagon is too heavy," he said. "The oxen are very tired. They cannot pull such a heavy load over the mountains."

He took a trunk of clothes and then a barrel of dishes out of the wagon and put them beside the trail. He did not want to leave them behind, but he had no choice. He had to lighten the load. Then he looked at the big brass school bell. Maybe they could leave that here, too.

He turned to Grandmother and asked gently, "Must we keep the bell?" Grandmother looked up at him, tears slowly running down her cheeks. They had walked all the way from Missouri and had brought only what they could carry in the wagon. This bell was special and she would not leave it behind. Very softly she said, "Yes, we are keeping the bell."

Grandfather knew better than to argue with Grandmother when her mind was set. He climbed into the wagon again, bumped his head on the bell, and threw out the box of silverware instead. The box was very heavy.

"There!" he said as he climbed down. "That should do it." Why was she so stubborn about the bell? It was not as important as the seedlings, packed carefully in a barrel. They would plant those seedlings and someday they would have orchards full of apple trees, with lots of delicious apples.

Grandmother looked at the bell and thought of all the children she had taught. She could almost see them running toward the school as she rang that bell. And the sound was so loud it could be heard a mile away! No one in the wagon train had heard it, though, for she had wrapped Grandfather's scarf around the clapper.

Just then Johnny and Crystal ran up.
"Grandfather!" said Johnny. "Can I ride Lightning?"
"Me, too, Grandfather! Me, too!" said Crystal.
Then she remembered her manners
and said, "Please?"

Lightning was Grandfather's horse. He was a very fast horse, yet he was always gentle with the children. Sometimes Grandfather would let them ride him, but not today. Grandfather was too busy and the horse was already tied to the back of the wagon.

Suddenly there were sounds of creeking wagons and loud voices.
"READY TO ROLL!" called out the Wagon Train Captain. Johnny and Crystal hurried back to their own wagon. Grandfather took his place beside his oxen with Grandmother on the other side.
"WAGONS, MOVE 'EM OUT!" The oxen slowly started to pull the wagons forward.
"GEE!" *"HAW!"* Soon there was a long line of covered wagons heading toward the mountains. This was the 140th day of their journey.

Johnny and Crystal walked with Father and Mother for awhile but they soon became bored and ran off to play. The wagons moved slowly and as long as the children stayed with the wagon train they were free to run and play along the trail. But they could *not* run between the wagons.

Their favorite game was Hide-And-Seek and there were plenty of rocks to hide behind. They *did* have to watch for snakes and lizards because they liked to hide in the rocks, too.

Johnny was "it" and had just spotted Crystal. She was backing up to a large flat rock. He smiled because there was a big green lizard sitting on that rock. He watched her back up to it and almost let her sit down. At the very last second he said quietly, "Crystal, do not sit on that rock. There's a lizard on it."

Crystal screamed, jumped up, and flew through the air. "Johnny!" she
yelled. "You almost let me sit on it! How could you?" Johnny was laughing
so hard he could not stop. "I knew it wouldn't hurt you!" he said. "It's only
a lizard! Tag! You're it!"

Slowly the oxen pulled the covered wagons along the rocky trail. Early in the afternoon the Captain called out, ***"WAGONS, CIRCLE!"*** The oxen turned until the wagons formed a large circle, then stopped.

Grandfather unyoked the oxen and led them over to the grass. Then he helped Father set up the tents, repair the wagons and grease the wheels. Johnny carried water from the creek, while Crystal gathered kindling for the campfire. Grandmother and Mother washed the clothes. Later they would cook rice, bread and apple sauce for supper.

Johnny unhooked the milk bucket from the back of the wagon. All day long the milk had been churning with the movement of the wagon and now it was butter. He took the butter to Grandmother and finally his chores were done.

"Grandfather," said Johnny, "I saw some grass by the creek. Can we please take Lightning over there? We've finished our chores and I think there are fish in the creek. Would you like some fish for supper?"

Grandfather smiled, looked at Johnny's father who nodded, and said, "All right, Johnny. But don't go too far, and watch your sister."

This was Indian country, but the Indians they had met had all been friendly. Grandfather knew that the children were in no danger.

They found a perfect spot. They could still see the wagons and there was plenty of grass for the horse to eat. They threw out their lines and waited for the fish to bite. Johnny took his harmonica out of his pocket and played a happy tune. Crystal liked that song and she began to sing.

"Flies in the buttermilk, Shoo fly shoo,
Flies in the buttermilk, Shoo fly shoo,
Flies in the buttermilk, Shoo fly shoo,
Skip to my Lou, my darlin'!"

Suddenly, Johnny's fishing pole almost jumped out of his hand. "I've got one!" he yelled. He quickly flipped that fish right out of the water and onto the grass. It was a beauty!

Then Crystal's line began to jerk! She pulled and pulled until she finally landed a very large trout, much bigger than her brother's. "Wow!" said Johnny. "That's some fish!" Now they had enough fish for supper and it was time to head back to the wagons.

They had just settled on Lightning's back when a hawk flew out of a
bush and startled the horse. He shied away from the bush and backed into
a large thorn! Lightning panicked. He wheeled around and started to run.
But the frightened horse ran the wrong way! He ran away from the wagons!

Johnny grabbed Lightning's mane and pulled hard on the reins, but the horse would not stop. Crystal had wrapped her arms around Johnny's waist and the faster they went, the tighter she squeezed.

"Hold on, Sis!" yelled Johnny, as the horse ran faster and faster. Johnny did not remind Crystal that this was Indian country.

Johnny pulled and pulled on the reins, but the horse ran faster and faster. Then Johnny saw two Indians in the distance. They looked different from those he had seen before. Now Johnny was really scared.

Young Sitting Bull and his father were a long way from their home and they were all alone. They were surprised to see children on a runaway horse.

"Eyacaha!" called out the father. Young Sitting Bull quickly turned his horse toward Johnny and Crystal, urging him to run fast.

Soon he was right beside them. Young Sitting Bull grabbed the reins and together he and Johnny were able to stop the frightened horse.

"Th-th-thank you!" said Crystal. She was shaking and so was Lightning. Johnny jumped off the horse and looked at the other boy. They smiled at each other as Johnny said, "Thanks!"

Johnny looked around and realized that he and Crystal were lost. He did not know which way to go. He did not know how to find his way back to the wagons.

Young Sitting Bull knew they were lost and he knew how to help them. He put one hand to his ear.

"Look, Johnny, he hears something," said Crystal. The children were very quiet.

Then they heard a faint sound. *"Ding-Dong! Ding-Dong!"* That was Grandmother's bell! Now they knew which way to go! *"Ding-Dong!"*

They waved goodby to their new friends and turned the horse toward the sound of the bell. As they got closer to the wagons, the sound became louder and louder. *"Ding-Dong!"* They were glad Grandmother had kept the bell. *"DING-DONG!"*

When they could see the wagons, Johnny took his harmonica out again. He did not want anyone to know how frightened he had been. He played cheerfully as he and Crystal rode into camp.

"Oh, Susanna, Oh, don't you cry for me.
I come from Alabama with my banjo on my knee."

That night the family celebrated! After supper Grandfather played his banjo and Father played the fiddle. Everyone in the wagon train had a good time dancing and listening to the music.

Grandmother smiled as she looked at the big brass bell. She was happy because her family was safe and soon they would cross over the mountains! Then their long journey would be over and they would begin to build their new home.

The End

Favorite Songs On The Overland Journey

Oh! Susanna

Stephen Collins Foster

I__ come from Alabama with
My banjo on my knee,
I'm goin' to Lou'siana my
True love for to see.

Oh, Susanna, Oh, don't you cry for me.
I__ come from Alabama
With my banjo on my knee.

It__ rained all night the day I left,
The weather it was dry,
The sun so hot I froze to death,
Susanna don't you cry.

Oh, Susanna, Oh, don't you cry for me.
I__ come from Alabama
With my banjo on my knee.

Skip To My Lou

Flies in the buttermilk, Shoo fly shoo,
Flies in the buttermilk, Shoo fly shoo,
Flies in the buttermilk, Shoo fly shoo,
Skip to my Lou, my darlin'!

Skip, skip, skip to my Lou,
Skip, skip, skip to my Lou,
Skip, skip, skip to my Lou,
Skip to my Lou, my darling.

Little red wagon painted blue,
Little red wagon painted blue,
Little red wagon painted blue,
Skip to my Lou, my darling.

Skip, skip, skip to my Lou,
Skip, skip, skip to my Lou,
Skip, skip, skip to my Lou,
Skip to my Lou, my darling.

Fun Facts From Johnny And Crystal

**Eya`ca ha!** - (aiya`kaha) Sioux word - "Look! A runaway horse!"

The States - the group of states from Missouri to New York that already existed in 1849

Emigrant - person who moves from one country to another. In 1849 the pioneers who moved from The States to California or Oregon were called emigrants.

Emigrant Trail - any of the routes the wagon trains followed to make the overland journey to California and Oregon.

Oxen - most popular of the animals used to pull covered wagons across the country. They were noted for their faithfulness, dependability and steadiness.

Humboldt-Carson Route - in 1849 the most popular entryway to California. This is the route taken in <u>Grandmother's Bell And The Wagon Train 1849.</u>

Sitting Bull - 1834?-1890; Native American Sioux Indian; Chief Sitting Bull. When he was young he was called Hunkesni, meaning Slow, because he took time to think before he spoke. Chief Sitting Bull was a famous medicine man and leader of the Hunkpapa Sioux Indians. Mostly reknowned for his participation in the battle of the Little Bighorn. Born in South Dakota.

Young Sitting Bull - fictional character.

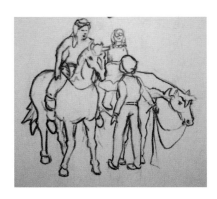

Discovery of Gold and the Movement West

Gold was discovered in Coloma, California, January 24, 1848. From 1849-1860, about 197,600 people made the journey from Missouri to California. The discovery of gold led to the opening of many overland routes. But people travelled west for other reasons too - - to find a better life, become farmers, plant orchards, or just to try a new experience.

The journey was long, difficult and dangerous. There was no turning back. Most of the emigrants walked the entire way, riding only when sick.   They travelled about 15-20 miles a day. It took five months to go from Independence, Missouri, to Hangtown (Placerville), California. A successful journey depended on good preparations, sturdy wagons, strong animals, good health, good guides, good weather, and being able to find grass, kindling and water along the route.

They travelled across Indian country. Many of the Indians they met along the trail were friendly, helping the emigrants if they were lost or in danger and trading with them. When the Indians began to lose their land, buffalo and food supplies to the thousands of people who were coming across the country, some of them became hostile toward these newcomers. Some emigrants were hostile toward the Indians, too. There were good and bad people on both sides and many misunderstandings.

Anything that was very difficult or almost impossible on the long journey was called "The Elephant." "I have seen the Elephant," said one pioneer referring to the Sierra Nevada Mountains (also referred to as "The Back of the Elephant"). Another "Elephant" might have been a charging buffalo or a major dust storm.

The family lived in a covered wagon for five months and that wagon carried everything they owned. Some pioneers started the journey with overloaded wagons, thus their wagons were too heavy. Family heirlooms were often found dumped on the side of the trail, especially close to the mountains. It was difficult crossing over the mountains. Sometimes the emigrants made pulleys, and pulled the wagons and animals up one by one. Yet they did it! Step by step they went over the mountains and conquered the Elephant!

Food For The Overland Journey

The following food provisions were recommended for two adults travelling from Missouri to California in a covered wagon.

20 gallon water keg
200 lbs. flour
5 lbs. tea
40 lbs. sugar
100 lbs. dried beans
8 lbs. baking soda
10 gallons molasses
8 lbs. cinnamon
100 lbs. dried fruit
8 dozen eggs (store in flour)

10 gallons vinegar
50 lbs. corn meal
30 lbs. coffee
20 lbs. salt
100 lbs. dried beef
40 lbs. rice
50 lbs. partched corn
2 lbs. pepper
60 lbs. pilot bread
20 lbs. bacon (store in corn meal)

All food provisions were stored in air and water tight containers.

Bibliography

Hunsaker, Joyce Badgley. Oregon Trail Center/The Story Behind The Scenery. KC Publications.
Hunt, Thomas H. Ghost Trails To California. American West Publishing Company. 1974.

Diaries and Journals

Brown, William Richard. An Authentic Wagon Train Journal of 1853 from Indiana to California. Edited by Barbara Wills. 1985.
Gould, Jane. The Oregon And California Trail/Diary of Jane Gould. 1862. Webb Research Group.
May, Richard M. The Schreek of Wagons/1848 Diary of Richard M. May. Rigel Publications 1993.
Smith, C.W. Journal Of A Trip To California. 1850. Edited by R.W.G. Vail.
Spencer, Lorenzo. Memoranda of Lorenzo Spencer in Crossing The Plains in 1852.
Warren Journal. Crossing The Plains in 1852.
Wonderly, Mrs. Pauline. Reminiscences of a Pioneer. Edited by John Barton Hassler.

Notes

Clough, Jack. Numerous notes and drawings.

Other books available by Joan Barton Barsotti and illustrated by Carol Mathis

Mike And Nick And The Pumpkin Patch
Nana Gets A Cat
Christopher And Grandma On Safari

For more information about the books, quantity orders or speaking engagements,
please write to: Barsotti Books, 2239 Hidden Valley Lane,
Camino, California 95709.

Acknowledgements

It is with sincere appreciation that I thank the following people for their help and advice:

Jack Clough, Trail Historian, Placerville, California; Member Oregon-California Trail Association

Raymond W. Larsen, Owner Larsen's Pioneer Museum, Camino (Apple Hill), California

Eleanor Barton Owen, my mother, for sharing her memories of her ancestors who were active participants in the overland journey

Ray Winters, Museum Technician, Sioux Indian Museum, Rapid City, South Dakota; artist; traditional Sioux name given to him as child - Mahto Wicha Kiza which means Man Fighting Bear

Written by Joan Barton Barsotti
Original oil paintings by Carol Mathis
Photography of oil paintings by Jim Ginney

Distributed by Taylor Publishing Company
1550 West Mockingbird Lane
Dallas, Texas 75235

Library of Congress Catalog Card Number: 96-085163

10 9 8 7 6 5 4 3 2 1
ISBN: 0-9642112-4-6 (Hardcover)

10 9 8 7 6 5 4 3 2 1
ISBN: 0-9642112-3-8 (Paper)